Rupert Bacon makes no pretensions whatsoever to being a newly discovered; A. A. Milne, William Wordsworth, Lord Tennyson, John Keats, Percey B. Shelley, S. T. Coleridge, Robert Browning, Rabbie Burns, John Masefield, or W. B. Yeats. He doesn't even aspire to be that prolific producer of the curiously varied output of masterpieces by the ever-mysterious Mr Anon. He simply enjoys making things rhyme in a rough and ready fashion.

If you have enjoyed this book of poems, he would be delighted to hear from you. He can be contacted by leaving an e-mail message at: themanwiththebear@outlook.com

RUPERT BACON

NOW WE ARE VERY OLD

Austin Macauley Publishers®
LONDON * CAMBRIDGE * NEW YORK * SHARJAH

Copyright © Rupert Bacon 2025

The right of **Rupert Bacon** to be identified as author of this work has been asserted by the author in accordance with sections 77 and 78 of the Copyright, Designs and Patents Act 1988.

All rights reserved. No part of this publication may be reproduced, stored in a retrieval system, or transmitted in any form or by any means, electronic, mechanical, photocopying, recording, or otherwise, without the prior permission of the publishers.

Any person who commits any unauthorised act in relation to this publication may be liable to criminal prosecution and civil claims for damages.

A CIP catalogue record for this title is available from the British Library.

ISBN 9781035861613 (Paperback)
ISBN 9781035861620 (ePub e-book)

www.austinmacauley.com

First Published 2025
Austin Macauley Publishers Ltd®
1 Canada Square
Canary Wharf
London
E14 5AA

Dedications

To Mr A. A. Milne and Herr Johann Sebastian Bach. Two chaps who perfected the art of how to entertain their audience.

Acknowledgments

As ever, the author would like to thank his wife for her tireless assistance in proofreading his writings. In the case of this book of poetry, she also had to ensure that the rhymes scanned cleanly as well as her more usual role as spelling and grammar checker. She is an invaluable part of all the author's efforts.

All drawings are by the author.

Three bears and one musical instrument have posed for some of the pictures:
Front Cover: Cuddles.
Lost Property: Noughty.
Teddy Bears' Picnic: Skip.
The Organ: Chichester Cathedral's Dr Arthur Hill 1888 Organ Case.

Table of Contents

Introduction	8
The Freeby	10
Lost Property	11
The Organ	12
A Summer Breeze	15
Entente Cordiale	16
History	17
Nothing in Life is Free?	20
Rum, Rum in Your Tum	21
Munro Mountains	22
St George and the Dragon	25
Ode to the Humble Worm	29
A Christmas Treat	30
Neighbours	32
Why?	34
Dear Deer	37
Ode to Loaves	38
Edge You Kay Shun or I'll Learn Yer	39
The Knight before Christmas	41
Sailing	43
Nicknames	45
Where are you going?	47
School Leavers	49
The Silent Ghost of the Night	50
Favourite Seasons	51
Teddy Bears' Picnic	53

Introduction

You might be curious as to where the title for this book originated. Sometimes a book writes its own title; for others the title writes the book. This particular volume wasn't like that and went through several options. There was the simple one of '24 Poems and Verses.' It was inferred to be in honour of J. S. Bach who paved the way for books based on two dozen with his '24 Preludes and Fugues' otherwise known as 'The Well-Tempered Clavier'. (Temper doesn't refer to having a bit of a strop in this instance but to a then new-to-him method of tuning keyboard instruments.) Title thoughts moved on to wordings like 'Poems for all ages' which morphed into 'Now we are seven to seventy.' For those of you familiar with A. A. Milne you will begin to see where I am going.

You see, it all goes back into the far distant mists of time when the author was the ripe old age of four and two-thirds and his Christmas present for 1964 was a copy of 'The World of Pooh' by Mr Milne. He (that is me, not Mr Milne, you understand) already happened to be familiar with the gentleman's works as he (me again) had taken a daringly dangerous and surreptitious look at his elder sister's shelves wherein lay two books of poems by old A. A. M. They were entitled; 'When we were very young', and 'Now we are Six'. You, being an astute reader, can now definitely see where I am going; 'Now we are very old' is an offering of humble homage to that pair of splendid poetry books. So whether you are a world-weary seven-year-old or a sprightly and young-at-heart seventy-year-old reader, please simply sit back and enjoy the silliness and fun of the rhymes.

Half a mo; another thought for those at the younger end of the spectrum. Although proclaiming aloud from memory with hands clasped behind your back to give your Great Aunt the pleasure of listening to you may have gone out of fashion of late, I can thoroughly recommend reading out loud to yourself, if you see what I mean. Not that I would also recommend you might shut your doors and windows whilst doing this; you don't want to embarrass yourself in front of the neighbours or your siblings.

Finally, this volume of 24 poetic offerings is not in the least bit sophisticated, nor I hope, is any one of them too clever by half even though the odd one or two have turned out a bit wistful, tongue-in-cheek or philosophical. They are intended to be just a bit of fun for you, dear reader, to while away a winter's evening and to dream of summers gone and yet to come. Their real purpose is to inspire the tyro poet, that is hopefully buried inside every one of us, just to have a go. To explain this better, there follows a twenty-fifth poem, free gratis, and for nothing. Please enjoy.

The Freeby

Poems for the young,
Poems for the old,
Poems to be sung,
Poems to be told.

Be they short, be they long,
They bring to life a jolly song.
Be they long, be they short,
A special rhythm in them's caught.

Some are simple, some are fun,
Write them down, let them run.
Of some one hopes they might inspire,
Though of silly rhymes, you should never tire.

If left behind a little earworm comes to stay,
Then the poet in you has earned his pay.
Once you're in the groove, out they pop,
I bet you'll find you just cannot stop.

Think of a subject that you love,
Let yourself go and coo like a dove.
Read them out loud, enjoy the sound
It's in poetry that life's truly found.

Lost Property

I'm looking for my bear,
it's an odd request I know,
but please help search both high and low,
for I have now tried everywhere.

I'm looking for my bear,
he's not an ordinary sort of creature,
he's very friendly but his extra special feature,
it is simple, he hasn't any hair.

I'm looking for my bear.
He went on a picnic to the woods today,
then he stayed a little longer for a play.
I've searched for hours and it just isn't fair.

That's him Officer, that's my bear.
Oh Horatio you gave me such a fright,
but now you're back the sun's extra bright.
You and I, we make a wonderful pair.

'Thank you Mr Policeman Sir', says Bear,
'You've looked after me ever so well
even though it was only for the shortest spell,
it's so nice to know that you care.'

Now it's off home to our lair,
Horatio's all in all my very best friend,
we're together again forever I intend.
Oh I do so love my dearest bear.

The Organ

He climbed the dust-laden spiral stair,
The sight caught him unaware,
Quiet it stood in its spacious loft,
With leaden pipes and cobwebs soft.

Above him the great beast towered,
A switch flicked, the machine was powered,
Pumps whined, the reservoirs filled,
His anticipatory senses thrilled.

Keyboards black and white awaited,
Stops abounded, their names all stated,
He opened a musical score
And selected pipes galore.

Krummhorn, Nachthorn, Gemshorn,
Gedeckt, Geigen and Shawm;
Trumpet, Trombone, Dulcet,
Tibia, Tuba and Salicet.

Koppelflöte, Waldflöte, Sifflöte,
Rohrflöte, Holzflöte and Spitzflöte;
Vox Humana, Voix Celeste, Melodia,
Vox Angelica, Viole Celeste and Dulciana.

Lieblich, Nason, Zauberflöte,
Clarion, Clarabella and Blockflöte;
Nazard, Dulzian, Sub-bass,
Salicional, Regal and Contra Bass.

Hautbois, Larigot, Principal,
Violone, Viola da Gamba and Cantabile;
Twelfth, Tierce, Nineteenth,
Dolce, Horn and Fifteenth.

Diapason rounded, Mixtures shrill,
Fingers' dancing, adding a little trill.
Deep Bourdon 32-foot pedal part,
Bach's musical genius, oh such art.

Toccata, Fantasia, Prelude and Fugue,
He could not stop playing, it would be rude.
Keys Sharp and Flat, Major and Minor,
Every glorious note couldn't have been finer.

Andante, Largo, Allegro and Vivace,
He was keeping up a tremendous pace.
Breves, semi and whole, Quavers all in a run,
Listeners could tell he was having some fun.

Out the sound poured into the hall,
Chord after chord from the instrument so tall,
Soft Flutes, deep reverberating Reed,
On such music surely God could feed.

Each pipe gave its sound,
Every note its place had found,
With final crescendo and tempo descending,
A crashing finishing chord marked the ending.

As the last echo faded and was still,
Music no longer carried by the player's will,
The mighty musical machine seemed dead,
But wait, some other player will give it its head.

Music again will dance about,
To put lows and fears to rout.
The organ only needs to let rip,
For music lovers to shout hip, hip.

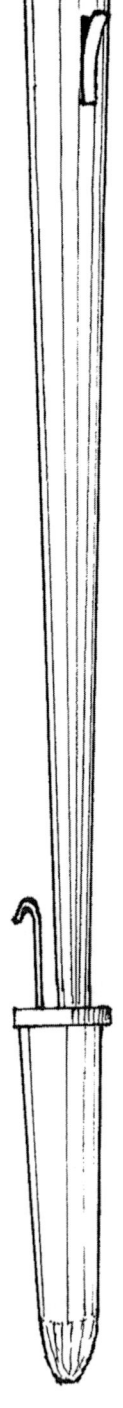

A Summer Breeze

I sat amongst the silent grass one sunny day,
So still and hot, even insects did not play.
There came a summer breeze; soft, gentle, kind,
It caressed and soothed my troubled mind,
The sun beat down upon the ground where I lay,
but now I was cool in amongst the waving hay.

Entente Cordiale

They sit in the sun upon a bench,
The man and a very lovely wench,
He is English and she is French.

Little messages to one another they send,
Not a word do they comprehend,
But love's meaning's clear in the end.

"I say, old girl, fancy a cup of tea?"
"Mais non, un vin rouge peut-être, mais oui,"
They're getting there in the end you see.

He loves her, she has l'amour for him,
The relationship's going with pep and vim.
She'll be looking out her trousseau for to trim.

With one another in love united,
It's off to the church to be promptly plighted,
No language is required, you can see they are delighted.

Lifelong they'll remain a pair,
So you may walk by the bench and stare,
At the success of the perfect foreign affair.

History

Now please don't be furious,
I'm about to tell you something curious,
Kings come and Queens go,
Are the people their common foe?

By what right do they rule over us?
Just pay your taxes – do not fuss.
History is written by the winner,
They make their enemies the sinner.

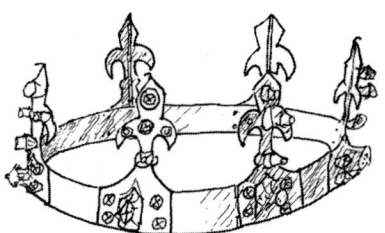

Let's look at a few examples for now,
But remember before each to bow.
It may seem a random selection,
But they're an interesting collection.

King Alfred, he might have burnt the cakes,
But he'll have been a dab hand with well-done steaks.
Canute lost a fight with the sea,
Yet there he is on the royal family tree.

William number one killed Harold,
So onto England's throne he barrelled.
King John was not bad but kind,
Look it up, it is truth you *may* find.

'Hunchback' Richard the Third,
Was a jolly good chap I've also heard.
Henry the Eighth, six wives he had,
Big of him or, for them, was it sad?

Guy Fawkes, under leaders he lit a fuse,
He failed; Heads you win, tails you lose,
George the Third was apparently mad,
But who's to say that's all bad.

Victoria reigned for ages and ages,
Her doings filled pages and pages.
George the Sixth had a terrible stutter,
Good he was but still the people mutter.

Charles the Third, our present king,
He's brilliant, just the thing.
Is he an exception to history?
Queen Camilla is sure to agree.

Some are good, some are bad,
Some are happy, some are sad.
So it goes on through time,
It's the way it is, that's fine.

Royalty seems to carry on and on,
But one day all sovereigns will be gone.
The world will eventually stop,
And then you, me and them, off we pop.

All are equal at the very end,
Our crimes we cannot defend.
A greater judgement is to come,
Then we are all the fools, everyone.

For you see there is a King I've heard tell,
Who'd like to get to know you very well.
Long, long ago He was born in a stable,
He tried to explain His message of love but wasn't able.

His people turned upon Him, said 'poo to you and fie',
They nailed Him to a cross and left Him there to die.
But death couldn't keep Him down,
So He's alive for ever with His crown.

He still wants to tell of His love for you,
He's a good man and a good King too.
Let Him hold the tiller, put Him on your helm,
We'll all then meet one day in His heavenly realm.

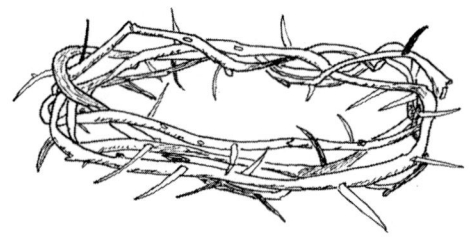

Nothing in Life is Free?

Lying with ones back couched upon the soft springy downland turf
with the warm sun upon your front, at your back the earth.
Watching fluffy white clouds drifting by in a brilliant heaven blue,
listening to skylarks far above singing out their everlasting songs to you.
The gentle breeze rustling amongst the beech leaves green,
the smell of fresh-mown hay drifting up from the valley unseen.
Ah yes, these things are free, they are things of God's giving,
experience each just once and you are truly living.
Who says 'nothing in life is free'?
Certainly not me, I do so disagree.

Rum, Rum in Your Tum

Pirates love a drop or two,
So do I, surely so do you.
Knock it back, pour it in,
It's so tasty, better than gin.
Strong, thick, and dark,
Raise a glass and hark,
Is that the sound of singing,
Across the waters winging?

Buccaneers one and all start to sleep,
Dreaming of their treasures buried deep.
But they're not worried and will not tell
of a map where 'x' marks the treasure well.
The excise men haven't a clue,
So they'll never pay them what is due.
Just sing and shout so very bold,
For they have silver and plenty of gold.

Doubloon, Diamond and Ducat,
Stored away in many a chest and bucket.
Pearls, Rubies, Sovereigns, Pieces of Eight,
Count it, there's an easy hundredweight.
Find it, dig it up when there's a need,
Meanwhile we will drink, party and feed.
'Rum, rum in our tum,
Sing on, let's have some fun!'

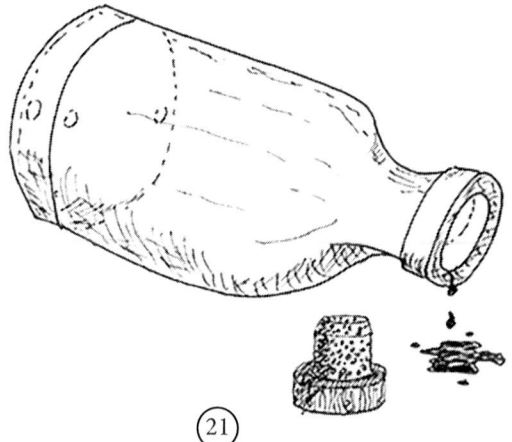

Munro Mountains

A Munro holds a mighty ascent in store,
It's a mountain of three thousand feet or more.
If you choose to climb and tick them off your list,
Just make sure you don't do it in the mist.
Terrain is rough and sides are steep,
So in your pocket Kendal Mint Cake keep.
But whether the weather be fine or bad,
Do them while you're young my lass and lad.

Scotland is the Munro's place of birth,
In that country there is no dearth.
Two hundred and eighty-two there are,
Many more than England and Wales by far.
Though named Furths south of the border,
To scale they're still a pretty tall order.
The land of the Dragon has a mere fifteen to its name,
The proud Lion can boast of only six, it's hardly fame.

The highest in the northern realm is Ben Nevis' peak,
4,411 feet, not for the faint-hearted or the weak.
Ben Macdui at four, two nine five, comes second,
Braeriach of forty-three feet less, third is reckoned.
Lovely Cairn Gorm stands at 4,084 feet,
It's only sixth but still it's steep.
Little Beinn Teallach at 3,001 may be short,
But upon the list by one foot it has fought.

BEN NEVIS

All around the Cardinal points they stand,
For the bagger there's always one at hand.
The massive mountains spin about the compass card,
To climb Schiehallion, the centre point, is pretty hard.
Ben Hope is by far the northern most,
And Ben Lomond guards the southern post,
To the west Sgùrr na Banachdich stands upon the Isle of Skye,
Over in the distant east, Mount Keen is 3,081 feet high.

SNOWDON

In Wales, 3,012 feet little Tryfan marks the start,
Snowdon at three, five six 'o' feet stands apart.
All of England's six, in the Lakes they tower,
Under great Scafell Pike the rest do cower.
Helvellyn to tourists is a well-known sight,
And I'll Crag is only a slightly lesser height.
Though Skiddaw is the shortest the district has to boast,
They're all worth a raise of the glass in a toast.

SCAFELL

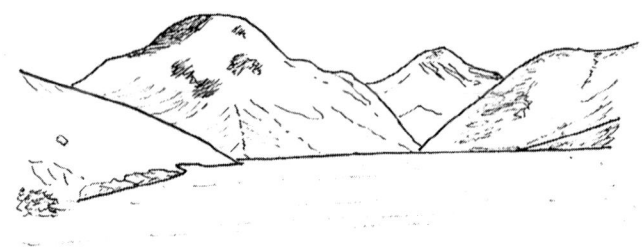

The Munro Baggers clamber and climb to the tops,
Then dash across the intervening land in bounds and hops,
Even though all our mountains to the Alps may seem tame,
To add yet another British peak beneath their belt is their aim.
So to England, Wales or Scotland go,
Above the magic line get your toe.
Bag them all if you really must,
But check the kit and in God put your trust.

Munros tall, Munros short,
Tick them off, it's a battle fought.
Romp the mountains, walk the moors,
Kick off the boots, bathe your sores.
Up you've gone, then back down,
Won the cup, worn the crown.
Come home safe, in you stagger,
Coil your ropes, you're a Munro Bagger.

St George and the Dragon

Brave St George in shining armour went out to fight,
Even though it was upon a dark and very stormy night.
It all began with local yokels round their tables seated,
"Something must be done and soon," they'd all bleated.
On they went, "It's not right, it's not fair,
Do something someone, does no one care?
SOS, our lives are in the most desperate danger,
When you need them, where's the bold brave stranger?"
For you see a dragon, they said, had burnt the village to the ground.
St George then appeared, "Tut, tut, this will not do, your story does astound."

So here he was upon his charger riding,
Up ahead were orange flames for his guiding.
The horse, though strong and very bold,
Shied and pranced for he was tired and old.
Great gobbets of fire soared high, he became afeared
You couldn't really blame him when he reared.
St George was down upon the burning ground,
His heavy armour pinned him there he found.

A great green, glistening, gleaming, grinning dragon sidled up,
On stealthy tippy-toes he approached the tinnéd goods for to sup.
Fire dripping jaws came close to St George's face,
Sweat was upon the knight's brow, his heart did race.
"I have no doubt it will be over very, very soon,
Let me be brave," he prayed, "do not let me swoon."
Despite his prayers before his end still he did a tremble,
And a repentant list of sins did he assemble.

St George wasn't really in a state to take the coming shock,
For the dragon did speak, "Good evening dear knight, watcha cock,
You're in a spot of bother like a beetle on its back,
And it looks like rains acoming, I'll lend you my ancient mac.
Do you know, lying there you don't half look ever so lazy,
Come on you, old boy, take my claw and, upsadaisy.
Though all these fires I've accidentally started,
They'll be out long before you've departed,
For it occurs to me, would you care to join me for to dine?
I've got barbequed sheep, pig, cow and lashings of chambrai wine.
It's not often I get the treat of a guest to host,
Maybe once a century at the very most."

Brave St George recovers his manners
As out his profuse thanks he stammers.
"What a kindly fellow you truly are,
Better than all those villagers by far.
I should be delighted to join you at your table,
But would you be so kind as to loosen my armour if you're able?
Even when eating the simplest of repasts in this iron vest,
It gets frightfully tight around the tum and upon my chest."
"No trouble at all old boy, there, the catches pop so very easy,
Out you step, that'll stop you getting a little queasy."

Saint George had made a friend indeed,
In the dragon's cave they had an excellent feed.
Good food, good wine, good cheer,
How silly, there had been nothing at all to fear.
'Fire breathing he may be,' thought the noble knight,
'But he's a jolly good fellow, I'm over the fright.'
"I say old chap, you've been so very kind,
Never before like this have I been dined.
It behoves me to return the favour, let's make a date,
I'm so glad we've met before it was too late."

Many an evening bash they had thereafter,
Though the villagers thought St George got dafter.
There was nothing they could do to stop the new mates best,
The dragon still breathed fire and St George wore his chain-mail vest.
Not that the varlets went on and on in undertone and mumble,
But St George wouldn't have it, "Oi you lot – you mustn't grumble.
I may be old and a bit of a duffer,
But it's your lot in life to suffer.
Just get used to a bit of trouble and strife,
The dragon and I are friends for life."

Villagers came. Villagers went. The dragon seemed ever younger,
So meanwhile each generation did more and more anhunger.
For you see, St George and his lovely dragon dear,
Every single night the groaning table they did clear.
Is there a moral to this little tale?
Yes; stay friendly with a dragon, do not fail.
Big appetites they most certainly show,
But if Saints can love them head to toe,
Then the least we lesser mortals should do,
Is in passing give them just a pat or two.

Ode to the Humble Worm

He burrows shallow and tunnels deep,
For the soil in good health to keep.
He's only long, thin and pink,
but his tiny brain does think,
'Keep on digging through the earth,
To glorious mud I give birth.
And keep down my little head,
As I aerate this flower bed.'
He's man's best friend the gardener does concur,
For compost in the vegetable beds he do stir.
"Stay down below, my helper dear,
For blackbirds stalk around I fear.
I'll hide you with some leaves araking,
Oh you splendid creature of God's making."

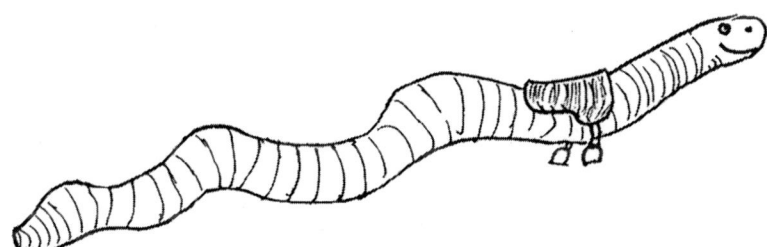

A Christmas Treat

With thanks to A. A. Milne for his inspiration concerning
the much-maligned King.

Bad King John was definitely not a good man,
Though all he ever wanted in his life,
Was a pretty, charming, and cuddly little wife.
But oddly on such simple happiness there seemed a ban.

As each end of year upon year came and went,
His Christmas list upon the mantle beam he pinned,
But all that came down the flue was cold north wind.
Did the presents come? No they were never sent.

His hair, that once was long and brown,
To grey it slowly began to pale,
I know this really is a miserable tale.
Will there be a happy ending for the Crown?

Then one time John had been so very, very good,
The Magna Carta he had signed,
On his oath to behave or be fined.
Surely it was enough to show where now he stood.

So one more go for happiness he tried.
Up went the list now so extremely short,
Come on Father Christmas, you know you aught.
Then in the morning, what's that in the sack he espied?

Something wriggled, something squirmed.
Good King John with faltering hand,
Undid the closing silken ribbon band.
Out popped a golden head well permed.

"Hello, I'm a Princess looking for a man.
Are you a lonely, handsome, darling King?
Please put upon my finger a golden wedding ring.
I've heard all about you, I'm your bestest fan."

Happily the narrator is so very pleased to record,
A charming, beautiful, smiling, loving Queen,
Now stands beside Old John, it's plainly to be seen.
Finally to good King John has come his just reward.

Neighbours

You've heard the Australian song concerning neighbours so good,
Well keep this under your hat, cap, titfa, chapeau, beret or hood,
For frankly such a beast is rarer than the teeth of a hen,
Let's enumerate for you why, in my fair hand and pen.

We'll start with the Aussie neighbours of the song,
The reason they weren't so bad is they didn't pong,
Being suburban they washed frequently and often,
So all the bad odours fell off as they did soften.

Now if those next-doorers had been from the sweltering outback,
Reasons to hate and deride them could have filled a very large sack,
Noisy, rude, crude, overbearing and boisterous, let alone the stink,
Would be enough to make an Aussie consider staying at home I think.

So how has this good neighbour nonsense come about?
Let's look at the history but whatever we discover, don't shout.
Our findings could be embarrassing to those next door,
Till now they've assumed your silence is because they're poor.

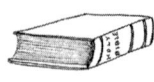
The oldest mention of these rules is in the Good Book.
Get a copy, read it, digest it, have a thorough look.
To pop on spiked shoes and from the neighbours to run,
You'll find these are no new feelings under the sun.

Commanded the book's splendid Hero; "Love your neighbour as yourself."
A too clever fellow asked 'who is my neighbour – what if he's an elf?'
The Hero replied; "I'll tell you a story to make it clear,
Though whether you'll listen is doubtful I do fear."

"There was this bloke what got knocked down upon the Damascus Road,
It was obvious he didn't know the foggiest about the Green Cross Code.
Fortunately for him a passing neighbour took a quick look; but then he moved on,
There followed a friend but 'oh whoops,' thought he, 'this is bound to be a con.'

At last a stranger stopped and stared; 'This poor chap's in a terrible mess.
I'll bandage him up and hope my good deed doesn't appear in the press.
They have the nasty habit of making a mountain out of a molehill,
I'd never hear the end of it but with good food this man *must* have his fill."

Jesus turned to his audience and asked,
"Who was a good neighbour? The friends that onward passed?
Or the stranger who stopped with purse opened wide,
Who didn't pass by on the other side?"

We know the answer. It was the stranger so kind,
He showed love and compassion, things of the heart you'll find.
But come forward in time, think of the here and now,
Nothing much has changed so in shame your head you must bow.

Today it is said a good fence is the best neighbour,
Even though building them is jolly hard labour.
Neighbours near or even neighbours across the sea,
Don't you just hate it when they're on the family tree?

Disputes, arguments, boundaries, branches and stray roots,
Stolen light, loud radios, bonfires, parked cars and dirty boots,
So it's off to the solicitors for a legal injunction,
Otherwise you're positive you'll never be able to function.

Cats' pooing, dogs barking, children in full throat,
They nick the TV, nab your gnomes or steal a winter coat.
What can you expect of their sort and type,
Who just want to get at you and have a bit of a fight.

But what if next time you have a deco next door,
Don't ask 'what can they do for me?' whether rich or poor,
Remember that old story above, 'love your neighbour' said God's Son,
Instead of friction, nip round to share and you might just have some fun.

Why?

Why don't apiarists play with apes instead of bees?
What does an arboriculturist have to do with trees?
Campanologists, are they boy scouts? It rings a bell.
Philatelists, what do they do? I stamp my feet, I cannot tell.
Why, oh why, oh why?

Ornithologists have nowt to do with boats and their oars,
Why do humans have hands and feet not claws and paws?
Why do pants and trousers come in pairs?
They're made all in one, it's really splitting hairs.
Why, oh why, oh why?

Does a parrot with psittacosis have a fear of the city?
In any case he'll not feel very well; what a pity.
Agoraphobia must be something farmers suffer.
Surely outdoor types should be tougher.
Why, oh why, oh why?

Why do birds live in aviaries,
Yet beavers don't live in beaveries?
Why don't lepidopterists have an interest in big cats?
Though oddly milliners don't mill but make hats.
Why, oh why, oh why?

Earthworms live in the earth and earworms in the ear,
But slow-worms are lizards fast and tapeworms spread from your rear,
Caterpillars aren't cats, adders can't count, robins don't steal,
Moles don't have blemishes and flies use their feet to taste and feel.
Why, oh why, oh why?

A meter measures but a metre is a metric measure you'll find
A yard's three feet or thirty-six inches too, what a bind.
A furlong isn't a hairy beast but an eighth of a mile,
Fathom's six-foot deep, it's so complex, what a trial.
Why, oh why, oh why?

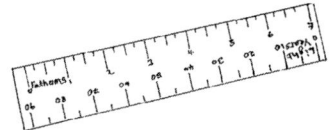

Why is the traffic stationary at rush hour?
What's the difference between flower and flour?
Karl Marx thought ticks and crosses equal,
Immanuel Kant *could* write many a sequel.
Why, oh why, oh why?

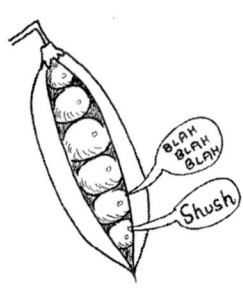

While Kings have a sounding kay and Queens are spelt with a loud queue,
Yet oddly with their knights, it's silent like knickers, knockers and knowledge are too.
Psychologists are full of wind and charge an enormous fee,
Though you may hear them fart, you'll never hear their silent pee.
Why, oh why, oh why?

Why is two plus two, four and not twenty-two?
Why is 'w' a double 'u'?
Yet an 'm' is not a double 'n'.
It's not logical is it then?
Why, oh why, oh why?

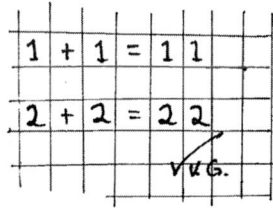

What makes aural to do with ears and sound,
Whilst oral is mouthed the same haven't you found?
A whole is complete but a hole is an empty void,
All this muddle leaves me right annoyed.
Why, oh why, oh why?

Why did the troll climb to his mountain home?
I don't know, why did he up the mountain roam?
The answer is one of the simplest,
He wanted to see if the view still *piqued* his interest.
Why, oh why, oh why?

Why don't teddies wear any clothes?
What; not even a pair of hose?
It's easy; because teddies are bare,
But hey, it's rude so please don't stare.
Why, oh why, oh why?

The English language; could it be made easy?
I for one, won or wun am feeling a little bit queasy.
Let's go back to the caveman days to grunt and groan.
Ugh, ugh, at last, I've got nothing of which to moan.
Y, O Y, O Y.

Dear Deer

What perfect, elegant creatures are the deer,
Amongst nature they really have no greater peer.
Stately Red roam upon the moor,
Spotted Fallow hide upon the forest floor,
Dainty Roe through garden go upon tiptoe,
Do keep clear of man, fox and every foe.

Great antlered Stags with bellows call,
Gentle Does snuggle amongst the leaves that fall,
Their ears aflutter in the autumn mist,
'Is that my husband asking for a tryst?'
Another glorious generation of Fawn is near,
What perfect, elegant creatures are the deer.

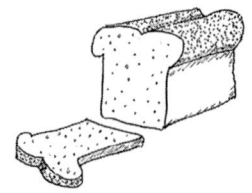 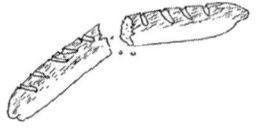

Ode to Loaves

White, Granary, Wholemeal or Brown,
Eat up your crusts and don't you frown.
Cottage, Farmhouse, Tiger and Cob,
Pile on the butter by the knob.
Poppy seed, Bannock, Tin and Muffin
Fill your face, go on, keep stuffin'.

Brioche, Bap, Bagel and Baguette,
All exceedingly tasty don't forget.
Sourdough, Soda, Scone and Spelt,
Warm them up, watch the butter melt.
Rye, Farl, Plaited and Malted,
All delicious and much exalted.

Now don't forget the Damper,
The staple of scout and camper.
Hedgehog, Sesame and good old Crumpet,
Make the dough fresh, knead it and thump it.
Tin it, leave it to prove, watch it rise,
Into the oven, eat it fresh if you're wise.

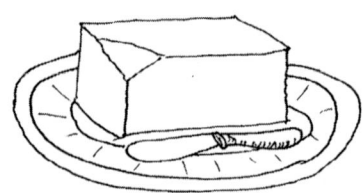 

Edge You Kay Shun
or
I'll Learn Yer

At school we go to learn our A, B, C,
Then it's numbers next; one, two, three.
Now add your money; pounds, shillings and pence,
Spelling comes after with grammar and tense.

Back home at last to watch at Mother's knee,
Or in Dad's shed to build a house in a tree.
Grandfather tells you tales of times old,
Granny wipes your nose if you've got a cold.

Oh! School's started again. D, E, F and G.
Four, five, six, seven, is that the bell for tea?
Only morning break for a quick play,
Then it's back to hard benches for the day.

Home in the kitchen, this is the way you cook,
Out in the garage, engines work like this, have a look.
Now let's walk the dog and feed the duck,
Dinner will be on the table by then with any luck.

On and on next day; H, I, J and K.
Eight, nine, ten, concentrate, no time to play.
"What do you mean you can't spell cat, dog and pig?
This is important yet you seem not to give a fig."

A bad report burns a hole in your pocket,
Will mum remove your picture from her locket?
"Oh dear," she says "what a shame but never mind,
I'll help so all will be well you'll find."

       L, M, N, O, P and Q,
   The teachers are in a terrible stew.
    Add, subtract, multiply and divide,
"Calculations in a mess; have you no pride?"

Family's coming round; you're home at last,
The evening passes in a flash ever so fast.
Mum and Dad telling how well I'm doing,
   They've a celebratory ale abrewing.

    R, S, T, U, V, W, X, Y and Z,
    That's the alphabet put to bed.
  Equations, calculus, logs and sine,
 I've not heard of them; is it a crime?

It's behind me at last; Dad raises a pint in toast,
 "Well done lad; I'm proud of you, I can boast,
Forget all that you never remembered to know,
You're fully prepared; out into the world you go."

So school was indeed an odd waste of time,
But I've learnt all I need at home; I'll be fine.
 I can cook, build a house and mend a car,
  It's definitely okay; I'm going to go far.

The Knight before Christmas

Once upon a time in a winter long, long ago,
There lived a Knight ever so bold,
But he had the most terrible cold,
He sniffed and snuffled but his nose did o'erflow.

"Try a box of tissues or some Balsam oil,"
His friends and relatives were full of advice,
"Fill the nasal cavity, stuff it with rice."
He dutifully did it but all was wasted toil.

December was flying and romping away,
His nose continued to stream and pour,
Hankies filled the castle from door to door.
Now Christmas guests wanted to stay.

He needed to get better to help entertain,
But then the servants and serfs went down with it too,
The doctor pronounced that it was a nasty case of flu,
Would they ever stop sneezing and feel well again?

Twenty-four hours to the big day,
No tree, no presents, no turkey prepared,
No tinsel, no streamers, nobody cared,
Sir Knight, staff and guests didn't wish to play.

Covered in snot, his armour had rusted,
"What to do? What to do? I really must get better,"
He fell to his knees as hankies got wetter.
So he began to pray, for in God he trusted.

His eyes were streaming and red,
"Dear Lord, dry up my nose, unblock my ears,
Clear up the head and staunch my tears.
I must improve but I can't go to bed."

His head nodded forward and visor clanked shut,
The clock ticked toward midnight so steady,
All through the castle nothing was ready,
Christmas would be cancelled; the unkindest cut.

Boing, boing, boing the clock struck midnight,
Christmas was upon him ready or not,
The lack of trappings mattered not a jot.
Prayer answered, cold gone, he could get on alright.

Up he jumped and praised the Lord, now he had a chance,
He dashed here and he dashed there,
Down to the kitchen and up the stair,
Quickly he prepared the Christmas castle to enhance.

That Knight was so pious and good,
He'd decorated the place from top to toe,
Cooked the feast and laid out presents all in a row,
Blazing fires crackled with freshly chopped wood.

He cheered for he was full of good mirth,
All was ready, the staff were well,
Relatives felt better and had a tale to tell,
On that long ago day of Our Lord's wonderful birth.

Sailing

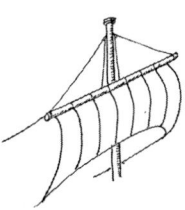
Cutters and Clippers sound like barber's kit,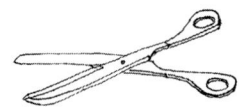
But boats and ships their description fit,
Likewise Sloops and Yawls are yachts as well,
You really don't believe me, I can tell.

A Barque isn't a dog's voice or a tree's coat
Like an Ark or Square Rigger it's a boat.
Hull shapes long or hull shapes short,
Starboard is right and left is Port.

Oh look at the Tender behind,
Oops, sounds a bit rude you'll find,
It's only a Dinghy though,
A Rowing Boat ready to go.

How many pints to the Galleon?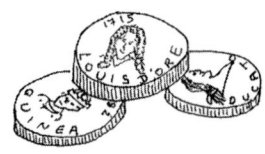
Is a Whitehorse a type of stallion?
Stow the first with a hold full of gold,
The second, give it a wave so bold.

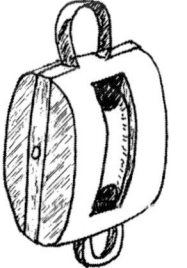
Don't start on a pulley called a Block or Sheave,
For sailors lace their lines in a complex weave.
As for ropes named Sheets and Braces,
To understand just drink rum by several cases.

Shrouds don't bodies bind,
But hold up Masts you'll find.
A Gaff's not a place to live or remark so rude,
Neither is Bilge talking rubbish all crude.

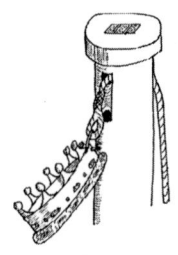
To canvas sails we now arrive,
They're what makes a boat alive.
Don't Jib at these in the Main,
Remember Spankers are a pain.

Staysails know not to budge,
Tow sails give the boat an extra nudge.
Mizzens toward the Stern do rise,
And Topsails crown the Masts in the skies.

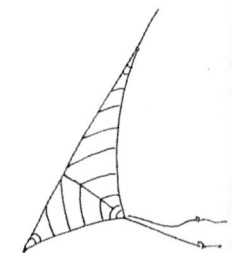

All shipshape and Bristol fashion,
We're ready to set sail and feel the passion.
Up she rises, down she falls,
Over the seas, the horizon calls.

Nicknames

Nicknames; some are kind, some are not,
Whichever way you look, there's an awful lot.
Of abbreviations simple there're quite a few,
Robert and Rob; William and Will; Stewart and Stew.
It's okay, the girls are not forgot, they get a look in too,
Elizabeth to Liz; Margaret to Marge; and Prudence to Pru
Man's best friend runs to fetch his stick,
Dog to Mutt, Cur or Pooch, take your pick.

What of our professionals so proud,
Is it alright to poke fun; is it allowed?
Doctors go Quack; a Sailor is a Jolly Jack Tar,
Officers are Top Brass, all the others, Squaddies are.
The Police do rather well; scarpa, it's The Law;
Plod, Copper, Fuzz or Rozzer to name but four more.
Even Clergymen don't get away with it,
Sky Pilot, Rev and God Botherer; they all fit.

Out in the rural countryside,
Many an odd name does abide.
Horses are Nags, Pigs are Swine,
Chickens are Fowl and Cattle are Kine.
Sheep have a lexicon all of their own,
Ewe, Ram, Lamb are perfectly well known,
What of Tup, Teg, Wether, Buck, Shearling, and Eve,
Mule, Gimmer, Chilver, and Hogget would you believe.

An Englishman's semi-de' is his Castle,
His land is divided up by the parcel.
He posts his letters in a bright red pillar-box,
Door rings, he asks 'who is it that knocks?'
Does he go to look, does he stir?
No, not he, such a plan does not occur.
Send Her Indoors, Old Girl, The Wife,
Better Half, the Mrs or Trouble and Strife.

We mustn't neglect the filthy lucre, dough or dosh,
It's a pound, not Quid, Nicker or Smacker if you're posh.
Lady Godivas and fivers are five pounds sterling,
Speckled Hen, Tenner or Ten, all are at the edges curling.
Twenty five's a Pony, one hundred's a Ton,
Monkey's five hundred and Gorilla's a Grand, such fun.
Don't forget to spend a penny or have a pee,
After your Cup that Cheers, Cuppa-Char or Rosy Lea.

Vegetables silently grow out in the mud,
The humble Potato is Tatie, Tater or Spud
A Fruity Gooseberry is synonymous to Goosegog,
If you're not keen on them, feed them to the hog.
Cows become Beef, poor old Lamb is a Chop,
Pigs make Bangers, there I think we'll stop.
Nicknames; some are kind, some are not,
Whichever way you look, there's an awful lot.

Where are you going?

Where are you going my little boy?
Off to play upon the barren heath,
with howling wind in your teeth?
Tell your old papa, don't be coy.

Where are you going my little girl,
Your hair in bunch and ribbon?
A visit to the neighbour is forbidden.
Tell your dear mama, my little pearl.

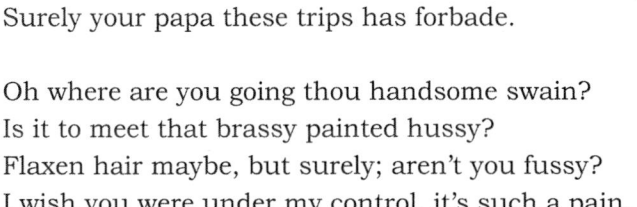

Oh where are you going my pretty young maid?
Is it just off to a country pub,
Or is it to a dubious nightclub?
Surely your papa these trips has forbade.

Oh where are you going thou handsome swain?
Is it to meet that brassy painted hussy?
Flaxen hair maybe, but surely; aren't you fussy?
I wish you were under my control, it's such a pain.

Thank goodness you're off my hands at last.
Son married to that nice wholesome girl next door,
Daughter to a man with prospects though still slightly poor.
I've almost forgotten all the troubles of the past.

What! You want us to baby-sit your brats?
I thought that was all left behind,
Nappies and tantrums, what a grind.
Come darling wife, we're away, I'll fetch our hats.

It's a bit of a laugh watching our children suffer too,
Just like us they're going through it now.
With badly behaved children so foul.
For there's nothing under the sun that's new.

Where are we going in our old age?
In sickness and in health,
To a cat's home goes our wealth!
And now at last we turn the final page.

Our three-score years and ten is little enough to show,
Like people gone before us, death is death and birth is birth,
Our fate is pushing up daisies from beneath the earth.
But hark; we hear Our Lord and Maker call, so up we go.

School Leavers

So you've finally left your school,
And think you know it all.
I hate to have to let you down,
Those 'ologies' are not the final crown.
Your troubles have only just begun,
There's ever such along way yet to run.

History, science, English lit and art,
Employers *won't* give you a start.
Maths, geography, English lang and sport,
They'll laugh you out of court.
'So you want to sweep the factory floor?
You'll need a degree, PhD or even more.'

'Are you still interested and keen?
You realise we won't pay you a bean.
Sure there's a pension scheme and sick pay,
But not for you, you're paid by the day.
Mind you, that's not an offer you understand,
From our premises you've been banned.'

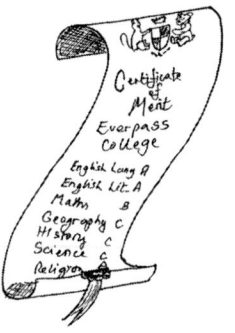

You passed the Os and As without one fail,
But down the job centre you must trail.
The patient staff assure you you're overqualified,
Don't bother with that lot; Oh, you've already applied.
They tell-you-off something rotten,
Pah! All that knowledge was best forgotten.

Fret not you young person about this farce,
Many a tycoon left school without one pass.
It left them free to go their own way,
Sure they struggled along with no pay.
But now they are each a household name.
Who knows, maybe you'll be the same?

The Silent Ghost of the Night

The master of the night,
Sails past in silent flight.
His talons outstretched before him,
To catch a mouse, with death so grim,
A beak as cruel as any raging sea,
He'll wait perched upon a swaying tree,
Until the moment comes to fly,
A rustle in the leaves, one more life passes by.
He turns for home in his lofty barn,
Where he preens his feathers soft as softest yarn,
The wind outside may howl,
But he's alright, for he's an Owl.

Favourite Seasons

Spring is the season of our youth,
Daffodils trumpet out this simple truth,
Even Robin Redbreast sings of it, forsooth.
Winter is firmly gone and past,
Everything is growing up so fast,
Lambs are born, fields are full at last.
Birds build their nests in hedge and tree,
They fly through the air completely free,
I love spring; surely with me you agree.

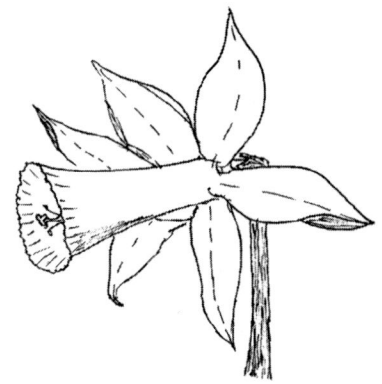

Summer heat brings on a drowsy feel,
Bees buzz, birds sing, church bells peal,
Hoe the vegetables, weed the flowers as you kneel.
This season is but a phase,
Stretch on out you sunny days,
Cloudless skies with a smidge of horizon haze.
Roses burgeon; yellow, pink and every shade of red,
Their heavenly scent fills the air and my head,
I love summer; all you do is admire the flower bed.

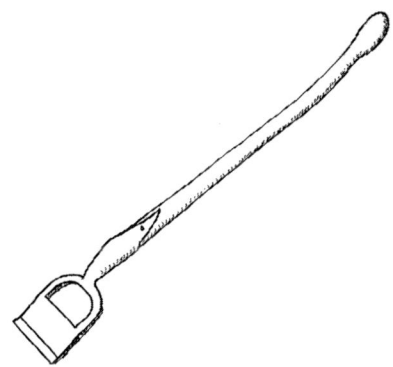

Autumn comes on with heavy dew,
Harvest home and apples quite a few,
It's the season of cider and hot stew.
Fill the storehouse with everything,
Swallows gather ready on the wing,
But watch out for the wasps and their sting.
Now the leaves are brown and gold,
Underfoot they fall to form a carpet bold,
I love autumn; its riches doeth me enfold.

Winter has come round again for to stay,
Naked fingered trees point at skies of iron grey,
Keep me safe Lord through the darkness I do pray.
Temperatures plummet as frost takes hold,
Light those log fires to keep out the cold,
Gather round and listen to stories that must be told.
25th of December and now snow blankets all in gorgeous white,
The moon is up and it adds its own very special kind of light,
I love winter; it is crowned by the blesséd baby Son of God so bright.

Teddy Bears' Picnic

Bears of fame there have been a few,
Jars of honey were enjoyed by one called Pooh.
Aloysius drank champagne so as not to get too fat,
Paddington's marmalade sandwiches he hid in his hat.
Baloo loved a prickly pear or pawpaw,
Yogi and Booboo raided dustbins for their food store.
Be it wood, beach or garden, day or night,
All bears love a picnic in which to delight.

'What of this poet's bears?' I hear you ask.
Where to start, that's the mighty task.
The bears I know and love in my home,
Clear the larder with a fine-toothed comb.
Be it savoury or be it sweet,
They regard every morsel as a treat,
But not for them a simple bun,
Oh no; a dinner party's much more fun.

Shall we start with 'a pair of teeth' appetiser?
Plain old sherry or cocktail well shaken, yes that's wiser.
Nibbles aplenty, sausages on sticks and cheesy straws,
Peanuts, crisps, savoury dips upon our sticky paws.
Twiglets, olives, pickled onions and the odd anchovy toasty square,
Devils on horseback and curried eggs make a nice combo pair.
Now lay the table with fine china and silverware bright,
Then light the candles with a glow so fair for tonight.

Fish course of smoked salmon and cream cheese tastes nice,
Or prawn vol-au-vent on a bed of very spicy rice.
Perhaps fresh caught trout in puff pastry to enfold,
Or a French onion soup if the weather's cold.
In summer a mini quiche and plenty of salad would be fine,
Ah, but what to drink, obviously a nice bottle or two of wine.
No, no dear waiter, that won't do, take away that plonk,
We'll wash this down with a crisp dry Sauvignon Blanc.

Bird course next we rather think.
Duck à l'Orange with meat so pink,
Partridge, Pheasant and a brace of Grouse,
Pile it on; this portion's not fit for a mouse.
Chicken drumsticks, wings or breast,
Creamy sauce over Quail's egg in the nest.
Raise a glass of sparkling Chardonnay,
Please top it up a little more I pray.

Here arrives the real meat of this splendid dinner party,
Beef en Croûte, Rack of Lamb, Steak and Kidney most hearty.
Roast potatoes and boiled too, parsnips and stuffing munchy,
Carrots, flageolet beans, peas and cabbage still crunchy.
Lashings of gravy, bread sauce, apple jelly,
Mustard and mint sauce to fill the belly.
Something bold and red should help us to digest,
Merlot, Bordeaux or Claret? All three I would suggest.

Stretch out paws, take off scarves,
We bears don't do things by halves.
There's pudding still to come,
Oh isn't eating ever such fun.
Light and fluffy, sweet and sticky, chocolate and creamy,
Meringues, roulades and treacle sponge puddings steamy.
Match them with a honeyed Sauterne yellow,
Fill my glass to the brim, there's a good fellow.

Is that a fully loaded cheese platter I espy?
English; Stilton, Cheddar and Melton Mowbray pork pie,
French; Brie, Camembert, celery, cherry toms and salt,
Cream crackers, water biscuits, oatcakes, butter; I find no fault.
A bunch of grapes adds a little treat,
Oh dear, I fear I'm welded to my seat.
Naturally there's an agéd crusty decanted Port,
Eat cheese without? What an extraordinary thought.

Brandy, coffee and wafer-thin chocolate mints,
Look at the cloth; it's covered in our paw prints.
We'll drag our stretched tummies up to bed,
I think it's safe to say we've been well fed.
You might think the end is surely in sight,
But tomorrow will be yet another bun-fight,
After a few hours kip it'll be time for a morning cup of tea,
We'll start over again; oh it's a Teddy Bears' Picnic life for me.